KEEP YOUR HEAD UP

WORDS BY ALIYA KING NEIL
PICTURES BY CHARLY PALMER

A DENENE MILLNER BOOK
Simon & Schuster Books for Young Readers
New York   London   Toronto   Sydney   New Delhi

First, this is for Derick Louis. Thank you for keeping your head up, in my class
and beyond. And this is for Derick's beloved brother, Anthony "Wing" Louis.
To all the men in my life who keep their heads up: Al-Tariq Dunson, Robert Tariq
King, Shareef Webb, Al-Tariq Dunson, Jr., and Cole Hudson Neil. Finally, to my
husband, Shane Paul Neil, thank you for keeping my head up too. I love you.
—A. K. N.

To my grandsons, my nephews, and all the little Black boys out there.
Don't ever let a bad day define you. We all have them. Keep your head up, and
I promise, you will get through it. You inspire me and I love you.
—C. P.

SIMON & SCHUSTER BOOKS FOR YOUNG READERS
An imprint of Simon & Schuster Children's Publishing Division
1230 Avenue of the Americas, New York, New York 10020
Text © 2021 by Aliya King Neil
Illustration © 2021 by Charly Palmer
Book design by Lucy Ruth Cummins © 2021 by Simon & Schuster, Inc.
SIMON & SCHUSTER BOOKS FOR YOUNG READERS
and related marks are trademarks of Simon & Schuster, Inc.
For information about special discounts for bulk purchases, please contact Simon & Schuster
Special Sales at 1-866-506-1949 or business@simonandschuster.com.
The Simon & Schuster Speakers Bureau can bring authors to your live event.
For more information or to book an event, contact the Simon & Schuster Speakers Bureau
at 1-866-248-3049 or visit our website at www.simonspeakers.com.
The text for this book was set in Altra Mano.
The illustrations for this book were rendered in acrylic on illustration board.
Manufactured in China
0721 SCP
Library of Congress Cataloging-in-Publication Data
Names: King Neil, Aliya, author. | Palmer, Charly, illustrator.
Title: Keep your head up / Aliya King Neil ; illustrated by Charly Palmer.
Description: First edition. | New York : Simon & Schuster Books for Young Readers, 2021. |
Audience: Ages 4–8. | Audience: Grades K–1. | Summary: D wakes up on the wrong side of the
bed, but discovers after a long day at school that while not every day will be a good day, the bad
ones will pass.
Identifiers: LCCN 2020021391 (print) | LCCN 2020021392 (ebook) |
ISBN 9781534480407 (hardcover) | ISBN 9781534480414 (ebook)
Subjects: CYAC: Mood (Psychology)—Fiction. | Schools—Fiction.
Classification: LCC PZ7.1.K5846 Ke 2021 (print) | LCC PZ7.1.K5846 (ebook) | DDC [E]—dc23
LC record available at https://lccn.loc.gov/2020021391
LC ebook record available at https://lccn.loc.gov/2020021392

I WAKE UP WITH MY HEAD DOWN.

No one said, *Good morning, time to get up!*
so I overslept. I'm kind of awake, but mostly not.

Dad tells me to hustle.
That used to be a dance
and now it means move fast.
But I *can't* move fast.

Because my sparkly toothpaste with the
not-too-minty taste is missing.

My sister used it to
make slime.

Toothpaste doesn't even go in slime.

I walk to school with my head up
even though I feel a little scrunchy.
It can still be a good day.

Any day can be good if you try.

But as soon as I get to school I am so mad.
It's Monday. I'm supposed to have on my gym uniform.

Now I can't play kickball!
And I'm the best kicker in my class.

I try not to
scrunch up my
eyebrows tight

or stick out my lips

or cross my arms
over my chest.

Maybe today I will be the Recycler.
That's a class job where you get to go for a long walk.
I like long walks. I can take my time and stop
and say, *Hi!* to Miss King. She always checks to
see if my head's up.

There is no long walk for me today.
Mia gets to go. I just know she's stopped at the cafeteria.

I tell the teacher Mia should be back,
but the teacher just says, "Stay on task, D."

In writing class, I get the last laptop—
the one with the sticky space bar.
Mia put a little dot with a marker on the bottom so she
knows not to pick it.
But I always forget to check.

In math, I say the answer before the teacher calls on me.
The teacher says my answer is right, but I am not right.
Because I didn't raise my hand.
Raising your hand is not math. Now I'm scrunchy again.
Miss King would say, D., keep your head up. So, I do.

It's Noah's day for show-and-tell. He has a rocket made out of a water jug. I try to help him bring it to the front. But then the whole thing gets smudged. I get paint on my uniform and the teacher's desk.

Now I feel like the thing that comes after scrunchy.
Because Noah is mad at me.
My uniform is ruined.
And the teacher is upset about the mess.

My mom and dad always talk about meltdowns.
A meltdown is when you want to keep your head up,
but it won't stay. A meltdown is when your face is
wet and your body is hot and your throat is scratchy
and you can't see well.

I have a meltdown.

The teacher sends me to the principal's office.

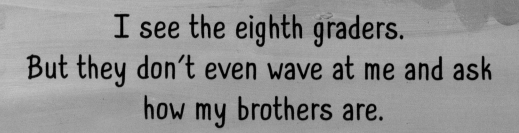

I see the eighth graders.
But they don't even wave at me and ask
how my brothers are.

I walk through the cafeteria, but it's empty.

I stop at the nurse and she
won't even take my temperature.
So, I walk to the office with my head down.

Miss King doesn't say anything about the meltdown. I always think she will look scrunchy when the teacher sends me to her office. But she looks like her everyday self. She has books and things to look at, so I just do that.

She has smooth round records and real turntables, too.

Miss King always says records are just like me: they seem complicated. But they're not, really.

You just have to be gentle with them.

You have to hold them the right way.
If you don't, they get scratched. And the
scratches are hard to fix.

My mom and dad come to pick me up. They look at
Miss King and they all have the same expression.

"Can I go outside when
I get home?" I say.

My mom says no.
We have to go to my
brother's soccer game.

"Can I use my tablet
when we get home?"
I say.

My dad says no.
It will be time for bed.

"So, this day won't get any better?" I say.
"It might. But if it doesn't get better,
what can you do?" Mom says.

I still feel scrunchy. But not too much.
"Keep my head up."
I say it, but I tell my mom and my dad and Miss King that I don't really want to. Miss King says that's okay.

I just have to want to try.